Cows in the Kitchen

illustrated by **Airlie Anderson**

Child's Play (International) Ltd

Ashworth Rd, Bridgemead, Swindon, SN5 7YD UK

Swindon   Auburn ME   Sydney

© 2007 Child's Play (International) Ltd   Printed in Heshan, China

This edition © 2013

ISBN 978-1-84643-621-5   HH1101138X804136215

1 3 5 7 9 10 8 6 4 2

www.childs-play.com

Cows in the kitchen, **Moo Moo Moo!**
Cows in the kitchen, **Moo Moo Moo!**
Cows in the kitchen, **Moo Moo Moo!**
What shall we do, Tom Farmer?

Ducks in the dishes, **Quack Quack Quack!**
Ducks in the dishes, **Quack Quack Quack!**
Ducks in the dishes, **Quack Quack Quack!**
What shall we do, Tom Farmer?

Cats in the cupboard, doggies too!
Cats in the cupboard, doggies too!
Cats in the cupboard, doggies too!
  What shall we do, Tom Farmer?

Sheep in the shower, **Baa Baa Baa!**
Sheep in the shower, **Baa Baa Baa!**
Sheep in the shower, **Baa Baa Baa!**
What shall we do, Tom Farmer?

Pigs in the garden, **Oink Oink Oink!**
Pigs in the garden, **Oink Oink Oink!**
Pigs in the garden, **Oink Oink Oink!**
What shall we do, Tom Farmer?

Goats in the greenhouse, **Meh Meh Meh!**
Goats in the greenhouse, **Meh Meh Meh!**
Goats in the greenhouse, **Meh Meh Meh!**
What shall we do, Tom Farmer?

Chase them away, **Shoo Shoo Shoo!**
Chase them away, **Shoo Shoo Shoo!**
Chase them away, **Shoo Shoo Shoo!**
That's what we'll do, Tom Farmer!